RIVERSIDE COU

A Note to Parents and Caregivers:

Read-it! Readers are for children who are just starting on the amazing road to reading. These beautiful books support both the acquisition of reading skills and the love of books.

 The PURPLE LEVEL presents basic topics and objects using high frequency words and simple language patterns.

 The RED LEVEL presents familiar topics using common words and repeating sentence patterns.

 The BLUE LEVEL presents new ideas using a larger vocabulary and varied sentence structure.

 The YELLOW LEVEL presents more challenging ideas, a broad vocabulary, and wide variety in sentence structure.

 The GREEN LEVEL presents more complex ideas, an extended vocabulary range, and expanded language structures.

 The ORANGE LEVEL presents a wide range of ideas and concepts using challenging vocabulary and complex language structures.

When sharing a book with your child, read in short stretches, pausing often to talk about the pictures. Have your child turn the pages and point to the pictures and familiar words. And be sure to reread favorite stories or parts of stories.

There is no right or wrong way to share books with children. Find time to read with your child, and pass on the legacy of literacy.

Adria F. Klein, Ph.D.
Professor Emeritus
California State University
San Bernardino, California

For Jim and Joan and all the Blackstad Bichons—J.K.

Editor: Christianne Jones
Designer: Amy Muehlenhardt
Page Production: Brandie Shoemaker
Creative Director: Keith Griffin
Editorial Director: Carol Jones
The illustrations in this book were created with watercolor and pen.

Picture Window Books
5115 Excelsior Boulevard
Suite 232
Minneapolis, MN 55416
877-845-8392
www.picturewindowbooks.com

Printed in the United States of America.

Library of Congress Cataloging-in-Publication Data
Kalz, Jill.
Tuckerbean in the kitchen / by Jill Kalz ; illustrated by Benton Mahan.
p. cm. — (Read-it! readers)
Summary: Tuckerbean has a fabulous time during his week-long stay at the Puppy Inn,
but his late-night activities leave him too full for breakfast, convincing the inn's owner
that he misses his family.
ISBN-13: 978-1-4048-2402-7 (hardcover)
ISBN-10: 1-4048-2402-2 (hardcover)
[1. Dogs—Fiction. 2. Cookery—Fiction. 3. Kennels—Fiction.] I. Mahan, Ben, ill.
II. Title. III. Series.

PZ7.K12655Tud 2005
[E]—dc22   2006009162

Tuckerbean
in the Kitchen

by Jill Kalz
illustrated by Benton Mahan

Special thanks to our advisers for their expertise:

Adria F. Klein, Ph.D.
Professor Emeritus, California State University
San Bernardino, California

Susan Kesselring, M.A.
Literacy Educator
Rosemount–Apple Valley–Eagan (Minnesota) School District

PICTURE WINDOW BOOKS
Minneapolis, Minnesota

4

Peni and her mom were going on a trip.
Tuckerbean couldn't go along, but he couldn't
stay home alone. Where would he go?

6

Peni packed Tuckerbean's stuffed squirrel and his snuggle blanket. She packed some treats that smelled like barbecue.

Tuckerbean was going to the Puppy Inn!

"He'll have fun," the innkeeper said. "Five days will go fast."

The puppy guests sniffed each other. They barked and licked. They played tug-of-war and tag.

Each night at bedtime, the innkeeper turned off the light.

But Tuckerbean was never sleepy. He slipped out of bed and tiptoed to the kitchen.

16

The first night, Tuckerbean chopped cabbage and carrots. He made a fancy salad. Lucy helped. She liked extra shrimp.

The next night, Tuckerbean made pizza. Nina helped. She liked a lot of cheese.

19

The next night, Tuckerbean baked a cake. He covered it with green leaves and pink flowers.

The next night, Tuckerbean filled taco shells with meat. He added beans and hot peppers.

YoYo cooled her tongue with strawberry
ice cream.

Each morning, Tuckerbean was too full to eat breakfast. Instead, he relaxed in the sun.

On Tuckerbean's last night, he grilled hamburgers. He fried onion rings. Lucy made shakes. She topped them with cherries and whipped cream.

26

Peni and her mom arrived the next morning.

"Tuckerbean wasn't very hungry," the innkeeper said. "I think he missed you so much he could not eat."

Tuckerbean winked and waved goodbye.
Next time, he promised, he'd make pancakes
and bacon or fried eggs and toast. Maybe he'd
even make waffles!

More *Read-it!* Readers

Bright pictures and fun stories help you practice your reading skills. Look for more books at your level.

The Best Lunch 1-4048-1578-3
Car Shopping 1-4048-2406-5
Clinks the Robot 1-4048-1579-1
Eight Enormous Elephants 1-4048-0054-9
Firefly Summer 1-4048-2397-2
The Flying Fish 1-4048-2410-3
Flynn Flies High 1-4048-0563-X
Freddie's Fears 1-4048-0056-5
Loop, Swoop, and Pull! 1-4048-1611-9
Marvin, the Blue Pig 1-4048-0564-8
Megan Has to Move 1-4048-1613-5
Moo! 1-4048-0643-1
My Favorite Monster 1-4048-1029-3
Paulette's Friend 1-4048-2398-0
Pippin's Big Jump 1-4048-0555-9
Pony Party 1-4048-1612-7
Rudy Helps Out 1-4048-2420-0
The Snow Dance 1-4048-2421-9
Sounds Like Fun 1-4048-0649-0
The Ticket 1-4048-2423-5
Tired of Waiting 1-4048-0650-4
Whose Birthday Is It? 1-4048-0554-0

Looking for a specific title or level? A complete list of *Read-it!* Readers is available on our Web site:
www.picturewindowbooks.com